Alaska,
Uncle Jim,
And Me

Alaska, Uncle Jim, And Me

by **Marti Arnold**

Illustrated by
April Dessereau
Marti Arnold
David Present

Fireweed Press

P. O. Box 6011   Falls Church, VA 22046

Published by

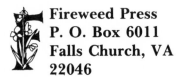 **Fireweed Press**
P. O. Box 6011
Falls Church, VA
22046

Library of Congress Catalog Number: 83-80267
International Standard Book Number 0-912683-00-7

Library of Congress Cataloging in Publication Data

Arnold, Marti, 1928-
    Alaska, Uncle Jim, and me.

    Summary: A young boy describes his adventures with
his Uncle Jim in Alaska.
    [1. Alaska—Fiction.   2. Uncles—Fiction]
I. Dessereau, April, ill.   II. Present, David, ill.
III. Title.
PZ7.A7364A   1983   [Fic]   83-80267
ISBN 0-912683-00-7 (pbk.)

To the real "Uncle Jim"

Acknowledgements

My gratitude goes to so many people. To Forest Arnold for his help in planning and editing the first painful drafts. To Marian Lesko for editing, typing, and proofing, and especially patience when I repeatedly changed my mind. Thanks also to my other readers for their helpful suggestions, especially Maureen and Elaine Adams, Helen Williams, Skit MacPherson, and my husband, Delbert.

Special thanks go to my illustrators. To the artist and sculptor, David Present, for his drawings, his enthusiasm, encouragement, and most especially for sharing the thrill of Alaska with us.

Many, many thanks to April Dessereau, the artist and teacher, both for her drawings and cover design.

CONTENTS

1

Me and Jim

My Uncle Jim is a great guy. I spend every summer with him, up in Alaska. He likes me too. He talks to me sometimes and he listens to me. Maybe that's because he gets lonely up there. I think he likes me because he likes ME, not just because my parents are dead and Jim feels he has to take care of me.

My Aunt Marge, here in Seattle, likes me, but she feels obligated. She never says it, and we get along all right, but she smiles too much. She smiles at me even when she doesn't want to, and she gives all my friends a big smile as if she thinks we're all great. . . . Jim isn't a smiler. He laughs, though. It booms loud instead of the soft way he talks.

It isn't just that Aunt Marge smiles all the time. It's as if people like her are trying to pretend that they care about ALL kids . . . as if everyone is the same. Well, I don't like all kids. Some of them are rats. I want to be liked because I'm a person. An . . . interesting person, not because I'm a kid.

I live in an apartment here in Seattle and that's not much fun for anybody. I really shouldn't blame Aunt Marge. I mean, how can she compete with living in Alaska, in a house, with Jim?

It's a whole different world up there, and folks in the Lower 48 hardly know anything much about it at all. I told my friend, Rick, about the questions people down here ask me about Alaska. He said grown-ups are really dumb. He told me that his mother got all mad because of a test she had to give her first grade class. It was made up in the Lower 48 and was the kind of test to see how smart the kids are. It asked the little kids easy questions about the moon shining in the sky at night and the sun shining in the daytime. The only thing is, the moon and sun act different in Alaska. In the summer it almost never gets real dark, even eleven o'clock at night or four in the morning. And in the winter there are only a few hours of daylight. Anyway, I've seen the sun and the moon in the sky both together many times, so how can anybody expect little kids to know something different from what they see and know is true?

I told Aunt Marge about that and she made excuses for the test. She makes excuses for everything. Jim doesn't do that. He says a lot of things are dumb and done wrong in the world. He figures you gotta do the best you can, yourself. That way you know at least one person hasn't messed up. And if you do mess up once in a while, he won't make a big thing about it. He thinks you should just try not to make that same mistake again.

Jim doesn't like me to act like he's perfect, or that he can replace my Dad. He says him and me are just buddies. Of course, that doesn't mean I don't have to do what he says, but mostly he doesn't tell me what to do. . . . Seems like Aunt Marge can find more things to tell me to do and not do. I'm at school most of the time, so I'm hardly ever here, and she works, so she's gone too, but when we are both here she can find more things to talk at me about. . . . Jim isn't a talker. When he does talk it's mostly to tell stories about things that happened to him or to someone else. Then he talks a lot. But he's not much for ordering me around. Not that I don't jump when he gives an order. If he ordered me to jump in the river in winter, no questions asked, I'd jump in. Only one time I didn't do what Jim said, and that was when I was only eight. . . . I don't like to talk about that, but I guess I will.

It was my first year to visit Jim. My Mom was sick. She was going to have my baby brother and was having a terrible time, always having to go to the hospital. My Dad had to work and there was nobody to stay home with me. Of course, I didn't need anyone to take care of me, but my Dad said Jim wanted to get to know his nephew, and that when Jim was busy Rick's Mom would look after me. Rick lives down the street from Jim. He's two years older than me and I'd have somebody to play with.

That was my first trip on a plane and I admit I was a little scared. I don't like being closed in places, like an airplane, and I was afraid Jim wouldn't meet me. Or maybe the plane would crash or something. I don't worry about things like that much now, except sometimes.

Anyway, Jim met me and I spent three weeks with him that summer. He treated me just fine. He does construction work, builds houses and things, and lots of times he took me right with him when he'd drive around from one job to another to check on his work crews. Other times I'd stay around and play with Rick.

I'd been staying with Jim about two weeks when it happened . . . when I didn't do exactly as Jim said. I was with him and he was driving down the road in his pick-up, when some darn fool in a car came straight towards us goin' a hundred miles an hour. The road was curvy and that maniac was passing a line of cars. When he saw us, he knew he could never squeeze into that line of cars, 'specially because they were goin' about 55 and he was goin' a hundred. It all happened so fast a person couldn't figure out what to do. But Jim's a fast thinker. He went right up on the shoulder of the road and got out of the way. The man who was driving so fast could have gone off into a ditch if he wanted, but he just kept goin' and hit the car coming behind us, head on. Well, those two cars went up in the air, like bikes doing a wheelie. Then they rolled together down in the ditch.

Uncle Jim was out of his truck in a flash, to help, and he shouted to me, "Mark, stay there". But I didn't listen, and pretty soon I got out of the truck and went over to see.

Jim went first to the guy who'd been hit. His head was bleedin' something awful, just covered with blood. Jim helped him out of the car and looked at his leg which was bleeding, and turned out was broken too.

That man was hurt, but he was cussin' up a storm. "Get my gun out of the car," he shouted. "I'm going to shoot that blankety blank who ran me down." Only he wasn't saying blankety blank. He was cussin', and I didn't blame him!

Of course, Jim didn't get the man's gun, though I guess he would have liked to shoot the man himself. He just told the guy to quiet down. Then he told a man in another car that stopped to go and call an ambulance. Then Jim walked over toward the car that had caused the wreck. Jim didn't see me, 'cause I was kinda hangin' back. But, like a jerk, I followed him when he went to help the man in the other car. It was too late for that man, and it was awful. The hood on his car had come loose, swung around like a big ax and gone right through the windshield. It cut the man in the neck, cut deep . . . so he never had a chance.

I was just a little kid and I stood there crying. That's when Jim saw me. "Mark," he hollered. "I told you to say put. When I give an order you've got to obey me." He was mad. I know he didn't want me to see those men.

Then he picked me up and carried me to the truck because I began shaking so much. I felt sick. I waited there until Jim finished helping the man with the broken leg, and the ambulance came and took him off. . . . Jim talked to me a lot that day . . . maybe to calm me down. . . . Maybe to calm both of us down.

You might think I'm making too big a thing over an accident that happened when I was only eight. Well, I'm not, and I'm going to tell you why. . . . Aunt Marge says I should talk about it. It's because one day that winter when I stayed home to watch TV, my mother, father, and new baby brother were all killed in a car accident. I never found out how it happened but I just prayed that it wasn't anything like the accident I had seen in summer. . . . Anyway, now you know why I live with Jim and Aunt Marge.

The natives in Alaska accept it if someone freezes to death, or is lost in a fishing boat, and I guess I understand how they feel. But dying in a car is something else, and I can tell you that when I'm old enough to drive I'm going to be the most careful driver you've ever seen. And you can call me chicken if you want to, but I don't care.

About Alaska, I don't mean to say life is hard like in the old days of the gold rush or anything. But it's different from here in Seattle. And folks who think the exciting times were all back in the days of the gold rush, well, they're dumber than I am, because lots of exciting things happen every day up there. Uncle Jim taught me that.

You just have to expect them to be different from what you read in most books. . . .

I know that seeing a moose is exciting. Once a full grown moose with two calves came wandering across Jim's property. I've seen lots of moose in lots of places, but no matter how many times I see a big old moose like that, it gets my heart beating fast.

Mostly I see cow moose, and they don't have antlers. But every once in a while I see a big old bull moose with huge antlers. Wow!

2

Fish and Fish Stories

Rick's father is a fisherman. Now that Rick is old enough to go with him I don't see much of Rick anymore. But I see him in August when the fishing is mostly over. The salmon run is early—in June and July, and when they're running everybody is busy day and night for a couple of weeks.

Rick and his father fly to Dillingham. That's a small fishing town on the coast. I was there once for a little while. You gotta go by plane, because there aren't any roads to get you there. Lots of places in Alaska—most of Alaska is like that.

Rick's Dad grew up in Dillingham. He's part Aleut. (You say it Al-ee-oot.) That means his folks come from the Aleutian

Islands. . . . You know, that's the tail of islands off Alaska. So he's part native. Lots of people think the Eskimos are the only natives, but they forget the Aleuts and the Indians.

It must be nice to be native or part native, because then you get to know all the old ways of doing things, and some of them you can keep doing. Like Rick's mother smokes salmon in their own smokehouse in the back yard. She's mostly Swedish, so sometimes I don't know if they do things like the Swedes or the Aleuts, but anyway home smoked salmon tastes good. Even in Alaska you don't see many people with their own smokehouse in the back yard, but me and Jim think it's great, and maybe sometime we'll do it.

What she does is cut huge fresh salmon into long strips. She leaves the skin on, puts it in salt water, with a little brown sugar, for about twenty minutes, and then hangs the strips on a drying rack, high up, outside, where dogs and other animals can't get it. The strips are like fat hot dogs. After they dry out a little, she hangs them in a tall skinny wooden smokehouse and burns cottonwood chips to give a smoke flavor. . . . In stores you buy things that are hickory smoked, but other woods are just as good. . . . I'll bet they don't even use real smoke in store bought stuff, probably just chemicals. . . . I have a cousin in Macon, Georgia, and he says the best barbeque is made from pork smoked with swamp oak. I guess that's pretty good, but I'll take salmon smoked with cottonwood any day.

Me and Jim cook a lot of fish. Rick's mom taught me to cook halibut. Jim doesn't like me to drink beer and I really don't like the taste, but Rick's mom, Mrs. Erickson, taught me to make a batter of beer, flour, and paprika. You dip big chunks of fish in it and deep fry it. Now that's good eating! It sure makes you forget what an ugly fish a halibut is. They're flat like a flounder, but bigger, with their mouth and eyes set on the head sort of crazy looking.

Jim cooks salmon. It's not quite as good as halibut, because sometimes it tastes dry, but it's still good. . . . I guess everybody knows about salmon and how they leave the ocean and swim for miles up stream, spawn, and then die. The female fish lays the eggs, then the males swim over the eggs and fertilize them. Well, sometimes the males get there ahead of time and wait for the females to come. That's what my favorite fish story is about.

Jim got to watching the big male salmon as they waited in the water for the females. This was in a stream way off from no-where. I wasn't with him when he first tried to do it, but Jim got it in his head to try and catch those fish by hand! He knew it was against the law to catch and keep salmon when they're ready to spawn, but there was no law that said that Jim couldn't try and catch them by hand and then let them go.

When he first decided to try, Jim told me

that he went in the water in tennis shoes, but the rocks in the stream rolled around too much and scared the fish. So he went in sockfooted, and that worked better. He sneaked up on a big old fish and started petting it on the sides. He knew you could do that to big old channel cats, so why not salmon? Then he grabbed him real quick, up by the gills, and tried to lift him out of the water. That old fish was strong. He pitched Jim flat on his face in the water—all 200 pounds of Jim, so that was a strong fish.

Jim said he tried it again, goin' in easy, sure that if he'd had better footing, he'd be able to raise that fish up. He petted it real good on the sides, grabbed it quick, lifted . . . and went smack on his face in the water again. He learned that grabbing that fish by the gills gave it too much power to swish with it's tail.

Anyway, the next time Jim eased in, he petted one on the sides again, but this time instead of going up toward the gills, he moved his hands back and grabbed the salmon just above the tail. He had the bend of the tail resting against the back of his hands so it couldn't slip through. He pulled that big old fish right out of the water! He tried it a couple more times and got real good at it, and the next year when I was with him, he showed me. . . . I've tried it a bunch of times, but I don't have the strength or patience yet. Those big males, if they rested on their tails, would come up to Jim's belt, and some even to his shirt pocket. Jim is over six feet, so I'm telling you those are big fish.

Anyway, what happened was that one day when Jim and me was looking the stream over during a salmon run, we met a game warden. Jim got to talking to the guy, wondering what he was doing with a fish net if he was really a game warden. The warden told Jim that he had been trying to net some of those big males to milk them of their sperm so he could bring it to the fish hatchery where they had eggs.

Now Jim sizes up a man pretty good before he lets on about anything. I told you, Jim doesn't shoot off his mouth. He talked to that game warden about this and that for maybe twenty minutes, with me dying the whole time, wanting to tell him that Jim could catch the fish by hand. But Jim had warned me never to interfere in his business, and not to go telling people everything I knew. So I just kept my trap shut and waited.

Pretty soon Jim said, "I can catch that big one over there by hand, if you'd like to milk him."

The game warden thought he was just fooling, and laughed.

"That's not illegal fishing, is it?" Jim laughed.

The game warden had been sizing Jim up too, and he suddenly knew that Jim was serious. He still didn't believe Jim could do it, but he knew Jim thought he could.

I was so excited I couldn't stand it, but I stayed way back so I wouldn't get in the way or do something wrong. I knew that Jim didn't get every fish he went for, and I sure wanted him to succeed with the first one.

He took off his shoes and went in sock-footed, easy like. The warden watched, still wearing a smile, still not sure about Jim. Jim eased on out in the water where a big king waited. Jim started pettin', glancing at the warden to let him know that he better get his container ready and get ready to help.

Sure enough, in a few minutes Jim grabbed and came splashing out of the water holding on to a fish that was almost as tall as me, right up to his shirt pocket. Together they got him milked, they moved fast, and then they let him go. Jim caught two or three more after that for milking, and the warden was really tickled with the whole idea. You could tell. Of couse neither of them wanted to do much talking about it, 'specially because the warden hadn't even been able to net one. And it was probably against the law to catch them by hand. . . . and if it wasn't against the law back then, it probably is now. So, let's say that's only a fish story, and never happened.

Everybody in Alaska seems to go fishing. I like to fish for graylings. They're like a trout but have a great big fin on top. They're fun to catch and good eating. . . . Jim knew a man once who had a fish wheel in the Yukon River. That's a great way to catch fish, even if he was sometimes bothered by tourists who took pictures of it and even wanted to go climbing on it. A fish wheel is a big wooden thing that you put at the edge of a fast moving river, like the Yukon. And the river has to be dirty as well as fast, so the fish don't see what they're swimming into. Anyway, the movement of the river turns a wheel that has sort of a basket on it, and it scoops the fish as it goes around, and then drops them down in the water to part of the trap. Of course, you may not be lucky and have fish swim where they can be scooped up, but it doesn't matter, because the thing just stays there in the water, going round and round, and you don't have to worry about it.

3

Winter

I've been in Alaska for Christmas holidays, but I never did spend a whole winter there. I spend the winters going to school here in Seattle, living with Aunt Marge, and the summers in Alaska with Jim. That just shows how crazy Aunt Marge is. She thinks that as long as I'm at school, she can take care of me, because I'm not left alone that much. But in the summer, when I'm not at school, she lets Jim take care of me. It never seems to enter her head that Jim does almost all his work in the summer, because nobody is building much in Alaska in the winter. . . . Jim is home most of the time in the winter, except when he's seeing his girlfriend, or hanging out at the

Gold Nugget Restaurant. . . . I wish I could live with him all year round, and go to school up there. But Aunt Marge says I'm a pest, and he couldn't stand me more than three months of the year. . . .

Anyway, just 'cause I never spent a whole winter up there, doesn't mean I don't know what it's like. It's not that different from other places that get some cold and snow. People still go out and do things. . . . They don't just hole up like a bear. And they get used to the days being short, maybe just four or five hours of light. And just because it goes down to thirty below zero or something, doesn't mean it's always stormy. You can still go out to a Pizza Hut or a McDonald's or somewhere.

Sure there's Pizza Huts. Did you think it was all wilderness? Well, Anchorage and Fairbanks don't look much different from Seattle. Not that big, though. Seattle is very big. . . . Jim doesn't like cities. We live far enough away from Anchorage so it's country, but still on a regular street with regular houses. . . . Jim built most of them for people. Built his own too. He has his own bear skin on one wall and has a big shelf on another one, where he keeps things. He has a piece of whale baleen that's as long as he is tall. Baleen is dark and stiff like plastic. Some whales have it in their jaw to filter out everything but the plankton they eat. Plankton is little tiny things in the water, really tiny.

Folks get used to places being cold and they know what to do. All the cars in Alaska have a plug sticking out the front. When it's winter, they plug them in an outlet on the outside of their house, and then the radiator doesn't freeze up. In fact, you can plug your car in an outlet on the parking lot of some big stores too. I've seen them in places like Penney's up in Fairbanks. . . . And you get metal studs on your tires to keep them from slipping on snow and ice. They're not allowed all year round 'cause they tear up the road. In the summer, I've used a special kind of pliers and pulled them out of Jim's tires for him.

Jim says you can't work outside when it's real cold, because you can't get yourself moving and thinking right. And it wouldn't make much sense to be building the outside of a house in the winter, anyway, when you can frame it up in the summer and finish it in the winter. Jim did put up one building when it was thirty below, and that was crazy!

The building was for some weather station, and it had to be smack on top of a hill. For some dumb reason, they didn't order the supplies to build it until December. But Jim and his crew went and built most of the building in spite of the cold, although they couldn't get it finished right away. Jim called the man he was doing it for and told him he wanted to take time to see that it was fastened down good, but the man said it might have to be turned just a little bit later on, to pick up the weather signals, and not to worry about it. Well, Jim and the crew got the whole outside done. Then they brought in the sections of sheet rock for the inside walls and leaned them against one partly finished wall, figuring they'd come back in a few days and finish up. It was bitter cold and a storm was coming, but at least the building was up and the sheet rock was safe inside.

Well, that storm raged for days, with lots of snow and wind. There was no getting out in the storm, and of course no way to get up that mountain. But things finally calmed down and the sun came out. So Jim took his truck to see how everything looked up there. He had to figure out when and how they could finish the job.

He couldn't get the truck all the way up the hill so he got out and trekked in the deep snow the rest of the way. The only thing was, there didn't seem to be a building where he'd put it. It was the size of a small house and even with the snow making everything look different he was sure that he was in the right place. The building had been smack on top of a very high hill, and that's where he was looking for it. Finally he noticed that there was almost a trail in the snow, not a footprint trail, but deep marks that went just a little way, disappeared, and then seemed to appear again just at the edge of the hill. Jim trudged over, looked down, and there it was. The wind had carried the whole building a little way and then tipped it over on it's side, just over the edge of the hill. He worked his way in deep snow down to it and climbed inside. After he got inside he figured out that the piles of sheet rock had thrown the building off balance when it went through the air, and then they had been enough weight to pull it down over the edge . . . or that building might have kept going.

Jim knew that there was no way to get it back where it belonged in all that snow, so he called the man he was building it for and explained the problem.

"Just finish it up where it is," the man said. "We'll worry about getting it in place come spring."

Well, it sounds easy, finishing it up just

where it was—except with everything all turned around, his crew was putting sheet rock on the ceiling . . . that was really a side wall. . . . But one way and another they got the job done and left it for spring.

Jim told me he always wished he could have been around to see that building moved into place and anchored down good like he knew it had to be, but he was busy on other jobs when it was done. Somebody did it though, because that building stands right on top of the hill—right where Jim wanted to anchor it down to begin with.

Let me tell you more about winter up there. I've been there a couple of times for the whole Christmas vacation, so I do know what it's like. We think the days get short down here, but up there it isn't even daylight until about 10:30 in the morning. Then the sun starts to go down about 2:30 in the afternoon.

In the winter, that's when you see the Northern Lights. It's also called the

Aurora Borealis. They're weird movements of light in the sky. Sometimes the light seems white, other times it's in color. It comes and goes and it's hard to take pictures of, but if you go to Alaska and want to see some great slides of the lights, they sell them at the museum of the University of Alaska, in Fairbanks. Jim bought me three packs and put them in my Christmas stocking one year.

I told you that Rick's father was part Aleut. When he was a kid he used to go to school by dogsled. Lots of people have different kinds of huskies for pets or even for dogsled races. Rick's father wanted Rick to have the fun of dogsledding so he fixed up a small sled that their dog, Zip, could pull by himself. He's a monster of a dog and probably could even pull a big sled by himself. And he's fast. They didn't name him Zip for nothing! The only thing is you'd get in that sled and he'd go off and you couldn't stop him. I rode in that sled a couple times and it was scarier than a roller coaster! And that was when everything went okay. Once he turned so fast it knocked the sled over and I landed in a snowbank. Old Zip heard me holler and came to help. He started digging and when he found me he showed he was sorry by licking my face.

I got to ride a snowmobile, but Jim doesn't like them. They are pretty dangerous because they go so fast, and when you add high speed winds to the cold and wind that's already up there, you can die from all that cold. Some places still have snowmobile races, but most of them have stopped. Folks get careless racing like that and can kill themselves just trying to win.

Before it gets too cold, and too much snow, people go ice skating. And there are ski slopes, and there is broom ball—they call it curling. So, like I say, you don't just hole up like a bear.

4

The Inside Passage

I like to look at maps. Geography is my best subject in school. Maybe that's because when I was a little kid Jim used to have me help with the driving by looking at road maps and figuring out where we were. Last summer we looked at road maps and figured out we'd been on almost every road in the whole state, except two —one going toward Dawson which is in Canada, and one down to Skagway. We decided we'd better finish seeing it all, so we took a trip and now we've been on every main road there is, and there are a lot of them. Of course, there aren't roads all over the state. Most places you have to fly to get to.

Alaska is big, and most folks don't know just how big it is. Shoot, I've even met grown people from the Lower 48 who didn't know Alaska was part of the United States. A lot of them didn't know Alaska was bought from Russia back in the 1800's by a man named Seward. Anyway, it has been part of America for a long time and was finally made a state.

But I was going to tell you about the ferry trip up the Inside Passage. Most folks don't drive the Alaskan Highway to get up there, they either fly or take the ferry part way. That's what I like to do. I take the ferry to Juneau, and then fly from Juneau to Anchorage, where Jim picks me up.

They call it the Inside Passage because you don't travel out on the open sea. You go along the coast, sometimes with a lot of islands between you and the ocean. It's also called The Marine Highway.

Those ferries are big boats. They carry lots of cars and people. And it's a long trip that takes three or four days and nights.

Last summer I was on the Columbia. Some people ride fancy ships like on "Love Boat," but the Columbia has cabins and beds too. But I didn't sleep in a cabin. They have a partly covered deck, called the solarium, on the back of the ship, and me and about 200 others slept there in our sleeping bags. There are heaters overhead, so you don't get real cold. The back end is open and you can wander around and see all the scenery when you aren't sleeping. It's great. I always make friends with people there. They feel that they have to look out for me because they think I'm just a little kid. Most of them are in their twenties.

This year I met a great guy who's a sculptor. He makes things out of fossil ivory. That's old ivory found on beaches that comes from walruses mostly, but sometimes from wooly mammoths and mastodons. (You shouldn't use elephant ivory, that's wrong, because then people in Africa would kill elephants just for their ivory.) Fossil ivory is nicer anyway. It sometimes turns soft colors like yellowish, brownish, or is streaked with grey. The sculptor carved a bird that had it's wings back, and there was grey in the feathers. His name was David, and this was his first trip to Alaska. I told him all about the ferry and Jim, and when we docked at Ketchikan for a little while, we went together on a tour of the town.

Later, at Juneau, when me and David said goodbye to each other, he thanked me for being such a good guide and gave me a keyring with a piece of fossil ivory on it. It had a picture of an eagle that he'd done in scrimshaw. I guess you know what scrimshaw is. Whalers did it for years. They scratched a picture in the ivory and then filled the lines in with ink.

I didn't know how I could thank David, and I never thought I'd see him again. But I did, and I'll tell you about that sometime. I was a good guide though. I knew all sorts of tales about the Inside Passage that I'd learned from an old fisherman, and I knew a lot about the little towns, 'specially Ketchikan because it's a neat place. There's one place in Ketchikan, like a park, where they have a whole bunch of totem poles. . . . They were moved there from other places so people could see all the different kinds there are.

Lots of them tell stories, but you can't "read" them. You need to know the story before you can figure them out. The one I liked best is the one that made fun of old Seward. He's the man I told you who bought Alaska from the Russians. He was the Secretary of State and he got the idea of buying it, and he did all the work. People thought he was dumb and they called buying Alaska "Seward's Folly." But buying Alaska *was* a good idea.

Anyway, one of the totem poles tells what the natives thought of him. They carved a high pole with nothing but a little man sitting on a chest, on top of the pole. That's all. Usually they have things on the bottom of the pole too, and sometimes along the whole pole. But they didn't think much of Seward because every time he came to Alaska to visit, the chiefs gave him potlashes and he didn't know how to act. Those are big parties, where everyone eats a lot and the person who's the guest of honor gets a lot of presents.

Well, Seward took all the presents, put them in a chest, and sent the chest home. But he never bothered to find out about the natives' traditions. He had a whole year to give a party in someone else's honor, and then he was supposed to give that person even more presents. Well, he didn't do it. So they gave him another potlash. And another. He was given five potlashes and each time he sent all the presents home and never gave the people anything in return. So, there he is, carved in wood, sitting on his chest, with nothing else on the totem pole because there wasn't anything else worth saying about him.

I don't suppose you ever heard of Ketchikan. Nobody has. But I guess you have heard of Juneau because it's the capital of Alaska. It may not be the capital for very long. There's lots of arguments over that. A few years ago the voters had to choose where they wanted a capital, and they picked a place called Willow. But that didn't end the arguments and the capital still hasn't been moved. Then I think they voted again and changed their minds. For one thing, Willow isn't even a town yet. Just about the whole town will have to be built from scratch. I suppose they should do it. It does seem silly to have Juneau be the capital when you can only reach it by air or sea. At least people could drive to Willow from Anchorage. . . . Most people live in Anchorage, so that probably should be the capital.

I like Juneau. It's a town that has a mountain behind it and hangs on the edge of the water. You can see the governor's mansion smack on the side of a hill, with it's big while columns. He's got a great view from there. Maybe he doesn't figure there will be a view like that in Willow, because it really does seem to be in the middle of nowhere. Maybe he just likes being on the Inside Passage. I can't blame him for that.

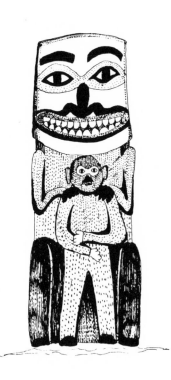

5

Jim's Tale

I've been talking a lot about Alaska, and I've even looked up things like dates so I'd be right when I tell them. But I think that things about people are more interesting, so I want to tell a tale that I've heard Jim tell. He doesn't tell it often, and I don't think he likes me to be around when he does talk about it. I think that's because he hasn't made up his own mind about how he feels about the whole thing.

Jim wasn't involved in what happened, although he knew everybody who was. One of them was Old Wilbur. He's dead now, and lots of stories have been told about him, but this one Jim knew about when it happened.

Jim was never a friend of Old Wilbur. Nobody was, I guess. The only friends Wilbur had were his sled dogs, 'cause he seemed to hate people. He'd almost growl at you, just like a dog.

I saw Old Wilbur on the street one day, just standin' off, starin' into space and some lady came up to him and tried to take his picture. He growled at her at first, just like a dog does, then he tried to smile and said he'd pose all she wanted if she'd pay him. He moved over to where she could get the mountains behind him, because he knew that would make a great picture. He really knew what he looked like. He looked like every dream you've ever had of some old sourdough. Somebody who's lived a hard life. He had a white beard and an old worn face. That lady took a lot of pictures fast, and she gave him some money, but I don't know if it was her pictures or some-one elses that made his face famous. Somebody probably saw the pictures she took, and then looked him up and took some more, and I bet paid him lots of money, because for about a year there his picture was everywhere and tourists were buying copies left and right. . . .

Anyway, I'm sure I told you Jim's work is in construction, and he has lots of guys working for him. Well, three of the guys up and quit on him once and said they were all going off to do some prospecting with Old Wilbur. Jim tried to talk them out of it because he'd heard lots of stories about how mean, even crazy, Old Wilbur was. Jim didn't trust him as far as he could throw a grizzly. But they said that no matter what Wilbur had been, this time it was okay. They had talked with two business-men from Des Moines, Iowa who had put up the money to pay them to help Old Wilbur. One of Jim's workers, Roy Baxter, had even been questioned by the Iowa men to see if he had the experience to test for ore. He proved he did. He was the old-est of the three guys who went, but they were all in their twenties, and were jack-of-all-trades. They knew some about mining, as well as construction.

Well, Jim couldn't talk them out of going. They thought he was only worried about losing good workers and wouldn't listen to his warnings. The plan was for them to be dropped off by helicopter with Old Wilbur, and his dogs, somewhere in the Wrangell Mountains. They were supposed to be looking for copper, gold, and other metals. Jim tried to tell them that even if they found anything there had to be a hitch to the deal. It would be almost impossible to get the ore out in that country. This was wild country they were going to, with no roads anywhere near. But they were excited about the adventure and so busy getting supplies together that they didn't listen. Anyway, they went. I didn't know anything about it at the time, but I knew that even a year after he got back that Roy Baxter would cuss like crazy if Old Wilbur's name was mentioned. So I figured Old Wilbur must have done something awful mean. Nobody had seen Wilbur since Roy Baxter and the others went with him.

Well, one day I was in town with Jim, buying some groceries, while Jim met some of his workers at the Gold Nugget Restaurant across the street. Suddenly I saw Old Wilbur behind me in line getting some groceries too. I ran and put our stuff in Jim's truck and raced to the Gold Nugget. Roy Baxter was sitting with Jim in a booth, but so were two other guys, so I just waited until they left. Roy was going to leave with them but I told him I had something private to tell him. We waited until just the three of us were alone in the booth, with Roy squeezed in the corner, next to Jim.

"I just saw that man they call Old Wilbur," I said, as if I didn't expect Roy to say anything much.

I was really expectin' some grand cussin', like fireworks on the 4th of July. But instead Roy started to shake, like I guess the earthquake shook. His hand shook so bad he had to put his coffee cup down.

"I'm going to kill that bastard," he said. "Let me up, Jim."

"Relax. Old Wilbur isn't going anywhere," Jim said. "He's moved back to the shack outside of town."

"I'm going after him, let me out of this damn booth, or I'll have to climb over you."

"You're not going to do anything to Old Wilbur," Jim said so quietly I could hardly hear him.

"The hell I'm not," Roy said, and he started pounding his right fist into his left palm.

"Have another cup of coffee," Jim told him. "No need to hurry back to the job."

"I'm going to get him. Hell, you know what he is! I should have killed him up there a year and a half ago."

"Maybe you should have killed him then, but not now. It's over, Roy. It's been over."

Roy calmed down a little, but still rubbed his fist against his palm. "I swore I'd get even. Every damned step of the way back I swore I'd get even."

"What are you going to do? Walk up to an eighty year old man on the street and hit him?"

"Don't give me this eighty year old man garbage. . . . You know what he is. . . . And you knew he was in town, livin' in the shack, and you didn't tell me."

"I just found out yesterday. Saw him walkin' down the road, with one of his dogs."

Roy looked straight at Jim. "Has he changed?" he whispered.

"Old Wilbur never changes," Jim said. "He hasn't changed in twenty years. Maybe fifty years." Then Jim laughed. "He still looks like everybody's dream of Alaska. . . . Alaska as it used to be, and still is, sometimes. Hard, strong. . . . He looks like a prophet with that white beard of his."

"You better grow a beard yourself, Jim," Roy said. He relaxed a little and stopped pounding his fist. "You were a prophet yourself when you tried to talk me and the other guys out of going. . . . Come on, I got to get back to work or you'll be docking my pay."

Then Roy got up and left, and I knew he wouldn't do anything to Old Wilbur. Jim had calmed him down. But I was dying to know what happened, so when Jim and me rode around in his truck that day, he finally told me most of it. The rest I learned since then, when he talks about it to some grown-up.

Old Wilbur needed money to live, just like everybody else. Nobody can live just off the land without having to buy flour, sugar, leather boots, and things like that. Maybe once, long ago Old Wilbur did raise his own food on his own land and hunt and fish for the rest. But somehow he lost the land. Some said he got squeezed out of it by the Federal Government taking it away from him for a park or something. Anyway, all he had left was a tiny plot with a shack on it, and his sled dogs. He was too old to work, and he didn't want to. He got along because he was smart enough to dream up schemes to get money and work out of other people. I don't know if he felt it was owed him, or if he just didn't think about other people.

Wilbur had met the two Iowa businessmen in a bar and got to talking about places only he knew about. Places that were rich in minerals, but he told them that he'd never had enough time or money to check them out. . . . If he could get some backing, he could make people rich on what he found.

The businessmen got interested. And who wouldn't when they'd talk to someone who lived as long as Old Wilbur and knew the country like few folks know it. All Wilbur really wanted was enough supplies to live in the mountains for a year or two. But he had to convince them that he was out to get them rich. That's why he said he'd need helpers, men like Roy and the other two guys who went, Bill and Sandy. With four of them going, they'd need a lot more supplies than if it was just Old Wilbur.

The deal was that they were to be dropped off early in the summer, and then picked up by helicpoter at the end of the summer. Nobody asked why Wilbur would need his sled dogs. Anyway, the dogs were his friends. But Roy wasn't his friend and he worked Roy real hard. Roy, Bill, and Sandy did all the loading of the 'copter, and Roy went with the first load to do all the unloading himself. Everything had to be stashed in a cabin that was up there. Then they all spent weeks and weeks getting everything in shape at the cabin, patching it, making it tight for winter. Roy even put a lock on the inside of the cabin door when Old Wilbur insisted. Wilbur never talked to the guys, never explained why it was necessary to fix up the cabin if they were only going to be there for one summer. And Wilbur never let any of the guys inside if he could help it. They had to sleep in their sleeping bags outside. And right from the first, Wilbur was cheap with the food. If they'd argue, he'd go inside the cabin and lock the door. Finally, they knew that if they were going to get enough to eat they'd have to do some huntin', which they did.

Well, after about a month they got the picture. Old Wilbur didn't care what happened to them. He had no intention of looking for minerals, and if he was careful and didn't share the supplies, he could live there for a year or more. They could half starve and wait another two months for the helicopter, or take off on foot for a couple hundred miles, plus trying to cross fast rivers. Roy got mad enough a couple times to think of jumping Old Wilbur and taking over the cabin himself. But Old Wilbur was smart. He never went anywhere without at least one of his dogs. The meanest one.

Then one day something happened. A wolf got in a fight with one of the dogs and half killed it. Wilbur came out and shot the dog, and then stood there looking at it. The three guys felt sorry for the old man, losing his dog like that, and volunteered to take it off and bury it for him. Wilbur nodded and let them know that they should take it off a good distance for the burial, which they did. When they got back they were quiet, wondering if Old Wilbur would treat them different now. He sure did. One by one they discovered that while they were gone he had stolen all their rifles and locked them up in the cabin. He didn't come out or even answer them when they banged on the door and shouted to him. He must have thought they were getting mad enough to think of shooting him. Which they were, but now without guns they had no protection against grizzlies, and no way of shooting game.

Roy had had enough. He was ready to leave. He said he'd rather walk to death or starve to death trying to get out of there than hang around any longer. And if they were going to make it they better leave soon because it would take weeks, and they could be stopped by early snows.

The three of them talked and argued for hours. Roy convinced Sandy that they should leave, but Bill said he'd survive where he was and would wait for the helicopter. The others didn't want to leave Bill, but figured he'd have the best chance of surviving around Old Wilbur. It wasn't that Wilbur treated Bill real good, but he was never quite as mean to him as he was to the other two.

Anyway, Roy and Sandy gathered up what things they could and began walking down out of the mountains. They were young and strong, used to the outdoors, and at first things went pretty well. The salted meat from the last deer they shot lasted a while, and Bill had given them the last of the cornmeal they got from Wilbur. In fact, it wouldn't have been too awful bad if they hadn't been stopped by a river. It was just running too fast for them to get across. They kept walkin' along the bank, hoping there'd be a good place to cross, but there wasn't any. Finally they spotted an island in the middle of the river. They would swim to it, floating their gear with them, rest a bit, and then swim the rest of the way.

They started way upstream, far up above the island because they knew that they'd be swept downstream before they could reach it. Well, they almost didn't get upstream far enough, and were plain lucky to reach the island rather than being swept past it. They were half dead when they crawled up on the shore, and they knew they'd never make it swimming the rest of the way across.

They waited until they were rested, and then spent all day and most of the night making a raft to get them to the other bank. Then they got some sleep and in the morning they took off on the raft. They had no rudder, just poles, which turned out to be useless in the current. They tried with all their strength to get the rest of the way across that river, but the current tore the raft apart and then they ended back up on the side they had started on! Most of their gear was gone and they were half drowned. Roy managed to keep his knife and he had a line with a fishhook in his pocket, so they were able to catch some fish to eat.

It had been raining off and on for days, but then the rains stopped. They watched the river, noticing that it was dropping down a little lower and was a little slower. They waited and kept fishing. Finally, when dark clouds began rolling in again they knew it was then or never. If the river swelled again they'd never make it. They swam like crazy, and this time they managed to get out to where the current could take them to the opposite shore.

The rest of the way must have been torture, and Jim never did find out who picked them up and where. Roy never talked much about it. In fact, when he and Sandy were picked up half starved on a road, they said they'd gotten lost on a huntin' trip.

Bill came back on the helicopter, without Wilbur. He was skinny, said he'd been sick, and he left Alaska the first chance he got. The other two, Sandy and Roy, finally looked on it as an adventure.

I've heard Jim say that he found out that Old Wilbur plucked a lot of pigeons in the way he plucked the two men from Des Moines. But they were asking for it, and they got their money's worth in adventure and daydreams, hoping Old Wilbur would make them rich. Roy, Bill, and Sandy got their share of adventure too, though they paid a high price for it. Jim seems to think that if you get suckered into a deal like that, it's as much your fault as it is the person who is treating you that way. . . . I know he never liked Old Wilbur, but how else was an old man like that going to survive in Alaska? Nobody was going to look out for him if he didn't look out for himself.

6

Denali And Bears

Mt. McKinley is the highest mountain in North America. I looked it up on a map and it's 20,320 feet. The other mountains near it are a lot lower. Mt. Brooks is 11,880 and Mt. Mather is 12,052. So Mt. McKinley really stands up there high and proud.

The mountain was named after McKinley who was running for president. A newspaperman who wrote a lot about the mountain when he first saw it, named it for McKinley. But native people called it Denali. That means "The Highest One." I think Denali is a better name than McKinley. It seems like a mountain's name should praise itself, not somebody else. 'Specially when the mountain is as grand as this one.

The name of the park where The Highest One is, used to be called Mt. McKinley Park. Now it's being changed to Denali Park, and I guess they'll change the name of the mountain back to Denali. Anyway, that's what I'm calling it.

You can see Denali Mountain from the highway, a hundred miles away. You drive up from Anchorage, past Willow, and then suddenly there it is, between the trees, and then smack in the middle of the road. It'll knock your socks off! At first when you see it standing so tall and far away, above the other mountains, you'll think it's a bank of clouds, because the top is covered with snow. Of course, you might see only clouds because there are usually a lot of them up there, even if the rest of the day is sunny. But if it's clear, there's not a prettier sight anywhere!

The rangers will tell you that most of the people who go to Denali Park don't get to see the mountain because of rain and clouds. I believe it. Most parts of Alaska, especially along the coast, or anywhere near water like Anchorage, get lots of rain. But—when you do see the mountain, and it isn't hidden, it's twice as exciting. . . . Christmas wouldn't be so exciting if it came every day.

Denali Park is where you get to see animals in the wild. You're safe from them and they're safe from you because you have to ride a bus along the only road in the park. You can get off the bus if you want to, and walk, or you can drive your car to a campsite, but you can't just drive around. If you take the whole bus ride, it takes all day.

The buses stop and let you take pictures, or just watch. You see lots of caribou, mostly in the big broad river beds. And you see moose, birds, even a peregrine falcon. And you see grizzlies. They ARE beautiful, but mean. Lots of them are sort of a blond color, and you see them wandering on the hills, digging for ground squirrels and things. They don't come close to the bus, like the caribou do some-times. Although I guess they could. One time last summer, me and Jim were just driving down a road, coming back from Skagway, and there was a young grizzly getting ready to cross the road in front of us. Jim stopped, because grizzlies get the right-of-way from EVERYBODY. The bear looked at us, looked confused for a minute or two, and then took off slowly back into the woods.

We were lucky that Jim was able to stop in time. We hadn't been expecting to see a bear and there he was, just after we turned a corner. I expect he was as sur-prised as we were. If we had hit him, he'd have wrecked the truck. Lots of people wreck their cars, even get killed, by hitting animals.

Bears don't see good, but they can smell you, or smell your food, so you have to be super careful when you go off hiking or backpacking. One thing rangers tell back-packers is not to wipe their hands on their jeans when they're out in the woods. You're supposed to wipe them on a bandana or something, and then put the bandana in with your food when you put it up in a tree for the night. . . . far away from where you sleep. Jim always kids me about bears eating me whenever I wipe my hands on my jeans.

We don't do much backpacking. There's lots of campgrounds all over Alaska and they're pretty safe. There aren't many motels and hotels, except in the few cities. That's why Aunt Marge won't go up and travel around. She said she'd like seeing the countryside but she doesn't like sleeping in a tent. And she's afraid to drive a big ol' camper.

People get killed by grizzlies. Even rangers. You can't predict what they'll do, and they move fast when they want to. Faster than you can run. Some kid at school told me once that you could outrun one if you were running downhill, because they can't run downhill fast. Well, two summers ago I went to Denali Park and watched a grizzly just strolling around the top of the hill. Then he suddenly decided to go downhill. He took off, and I tell you he could move! When I got back to school I told the kid about it and he said you'd have to zig-zag downhill. That way you could run to safety. I don't think I believe that.

Rangers tell you that if you surprise a bear, the best thing to do is not to run, but to talk to him calmly, wave your arms around, and slowly back out of his path. They know that works sometimes, but they don't know how many times it doesn't. And who talks calmly to a bear? "Hello, Mr. Grizzly. Nice day. You're not really hungry, are you? I mean, I'll go my way and you go yours. Goodbye old fellow."

They also tell you that you should wear bells on your legs, or carry a can full of rocks and rattle it when you are out walking, or do something noisy like that. Bears will hear the noise long before they see you, and unless you are between them and their cub, they'll stay out of your way. Maybe.

Jim knows a man who has a cabin near the Wrangell mountains. He goes there to get away, to hunt and fish. A while back he decided to take his son, and asked another man and his son. The boys were about thirteen and they begged and begged their fathers to let them pitch a tent near the cabin and sleep outside. The fathers didn't want to do it because it's wild country, but the boys kept begging so they gave in. They pitched a tent about fifty yards from the cabin, and they talked until real late, telling ghost stories and stuff. It was a warm night, so they pulled their sleeping bags shut, but didn't zip them up tight, and went to sleep.

They didn't hear the bear coming. All they knew was that suddenly there was a ripping sound as a full grown grizzly tore the whole side of the tent and knocked it down. It was half light, like it is in the summer, and maybe the bear was as surprised to see them as they were to be blasted out of a sound sleep and see him. Anyway, they didn't say, "Hello, bear!" They ran like the devil was after them, and it was. . . . They made it to the cabin too. If it had been a cold night and they had zipped up their sleeping bags they'd never have made it in time, because it would have taken a few seconds to get going. As it was, that bear hesitated two seconds while they took off like a shot, and he was right behind them when they reached the cabin.

The door to the cabin wasn't locked, because the fathers thought the boys might want to get back in during the night. If it had been locked, they wouldn't have lived. As it was, they burst in the room, with the bear right behind them, and managed to slam the door almost in the bear's face— and lock it. He banged against the door and the side of the cabin, and they began shouting and banging pots, until the bear went away.

That's one time when boys did outrun a bear, but they were darn lucky.

7

The Gold Nugget

When I stay at home, up at Jim's house, I take care of the vegetable garden and mow the grass. And I have to clean up the place and wash the dishes. Mostly, I read a lot and watch TV. And I like to draw pictures. When Rick is around we do things together. It's important sometimes for Jim to have me stay home and take messages about his construction business. Jim doesn't have an office. Most folks who want work done know they can find him at the Gold Nugget Restaurant. That's his office and hangout. He has breakfast there and meets his crews there. So does most everybody else around there in construction. Aunt Marge says that's a funny way to do business because she works in an office, where eveybody wears suits and ties. Jim hardly ever wears stuff like that. Even when he gets dressed up to go to Willow and see his girlfriend, he doesn't wear a necktie. He laughs and says he came up to Alaska to get away from neckties. "They're just a fancy hangman's noose around your neck," he says.

When I'm with Jim in the Gold Nugget, he sits in a booth and talks to the men. Everybody likes Jim and they come to him for advice. Sometimes I wish I'd get to sit and talk to him, but I sit at the counter and the waitresses kid with me. That's fun. When I get tired of waiting, I go out and sit in the truck and read.

Jim isn't rich, but he gets by. I've tried to tell Aunt Marge about how he does business, but she interrupts. I told her that unless he's doing a big job for a big company, he doesn't write up a contract. Aunt Marge said, "Oh, well, that 's the western tradition of honoring a handshake." But Jim doesn't shake hands all the time like businessmen do. He'll make an offer for work in that quiet voice of his, and he'll look you square in the eye to be sure you understand. If you accept his offer, he'll nod his head just a little, and that's the agreement. And he'll stand by that agreement no matter what happens. If there are snags in the job and it ends up costing Jim more than he could possibly figure, he doesn't change the amount that he agreed on. . . .

Once Jim made a mistake and forgot to include something. He wouldn't change it, even though he was losing money. I tried to argue with him that the man he was building for would understand if he explained it to him, but Jim wouldn't hear of it. "That was the price we agreed on," was all he said. When I tried to say more, he treated me like he does the folks who try to cheat him, who want him to do something for nothing. He gave me that look, not angry, almost a smile, but it says, "I don't have time for your nonsense." Then he walked off.

Lots of folks have tried to cheat Jim, and

some real deadbeats get away with it because Jim is too nice. That doesn't change the way Jim acts. . . . Last summer, an old lady came up to him just as we were leaving the Gold Nugget.

"Jim," she said, in her quivery little voice. "My social security check hasn't come. I just don't know. . . ."

He gave her an unusually big smile for him, nodded his head, and peeled off a hundred dollar bill. She didn't know what to say. She promised to pay him back, but he didn't wait around for her to say any more. . . .

Another time, I kept getting calls at the house from an old man that Jim had done some work for.

"The next time he calls, tell him that I'll put the bill in the mail," Jim said.

"But you never send bills, Jim. You usually just call people. I've got his phone number. Somehow you forgot and never told him how much it would cost."

"Listen, Mark, you tell him what I told

you . . . that I'll put a bill in the mail. He's old, maybe he'll forget about it. . . ."

"But, Jim. . . ."

"Mark, I don't think he can even afford to pay for the little job I did for him, but I'm figuring how to handle it. I know he won't take it free if he thinks it's charity."

Jim was right. After waiting all summer for Jim to bill him, the old man sent him a check for what he thought the job was worth. Or at least what he could afford. Even then Jim hated to take the money, 'though I know that on the same day he was taking out a short time loan at the bank, so he could pay his lumber bill on time.

The Gold Nugget is a busy place because Jim goes there. I'll bet if Jim started going somewhere else, the rest would follow. Of course, it's not just a restaurant for working men. Families go there and eat too. But they mostly eat in the dining room at tables, instead of in the booths or at the counter. Jim built the restaurant for Mr.

Dessereaux. He's part French Canadian, and a little bit Italian, so he knows how to cook all sorts of great food. He makes some sort of a thing called a crepe, that's filled with strawberries, and Jim liked it so much that Mr. Dessereaux calls it the "Jim Stratton Special." There it is, right on the menu, with Jim's name on it!

I expect Jim helped Mr. Dessereaux get started in business just like he does a lot of people. And I shouldn't be jealous because I have to share Jim. . . . I guess I really am a pest, and he wouldn't want me hanging around up there in Alaska with him all year round.

8

Aunt Marge and Uncle Jim

I wish I was as old as Rick. He works for his father. He works hard fishing, and they make a lot of money too. Fishing doesn't last long up there, but it sure pays good when you own your own boat, like Mr. Erickson does.

Me and Rick used to do lots of things together, before he started working so much. . . . But we had some fun last summer. We'd hitch a ride into Anchorage and spend the day there. They have movies at the art museum. They mostly show the old ways of the Eskimos and other natives. . . . The pictures hanging in the museum are nice too. . . . Jim likes pictures of real things, animals and all that. He has a great picture on one wall of an eagle, drawn by an Alaskan artist.

Aunt Marge's pictures are never of real things. They're just colors and shapes. She calls them abstracts. She says abstracts are more interesting. . . . The ones she buys are interesting, and I like them, but they aren't as exciting as that eagle Jim has. . . . She says that I can draw really good and she's going to have me take art classes after school. I guess I'll learn both kinds of art then.

I guess I've been bad-mouthing Aunt Marge. I don't mean to. She's a good person and she treats me awful good. It's just that she's so different from Jim, and sometimes I have trouble figuring out who is right. Like with talking. Aunt Marge and me both talk a lot. We talk about things that bother us. She says it's healthy. . . . I felt awful bad when I first came to live with her, because I lost my parents and little brother. I cried a lot. I couldn't even talk without crying. But Aunt Marge didn't try to make me stop. She'd cry with me, 'cause my mom was her sister and she missed her. . . . You wouldn't believe sisters could be so different. She doesn't even look like my mother. Anyway, I stopped crying and stopped talking and got to worrying. I guess I began to think all the time that if I hadn't stayed home to watch TV that day, maybe my parents wouldn't have died. Maybe I'd have seen the car that hit them, or maybe they wouldn't have been on that street. They'd have hurried home a different way so I could see that movie on TV. . . . I felt like somehow it was my fault that they were dead and I was alive.

Aunt Marge knew that I was worried and she made me say it all out. She told me that everybody feels guilty when other people die. She said it was a good thing to feel that way for a little while, because it was natural and showed I cared. It was an accident that just happened, and that I shouldn't worry about it anymore.

But, you know, grown-ups are funny.

Aunt Marge talks about everything except the man she divorced. She was married only a little while, when she was still in college. And Jim, he's divorced, and he doesn't talk much, but sometimes he talks about Sally, who he was married to. He met her on a trip to the Lower 48, years ago. He thought she'd like Alaska, and she thought she would too. But the longer she was up there, the more she hated it. And she began to hate Jim because he loved it so much. He says she was a "city person" and that's that.

Jim thinks my Dad was a city person and I think he worries about whether he's teaching me right. Maybe I'm a city person too. My Dad was a lawyer. Even when they were brothers on the farm, my Dad liked to read and study. Jim liked reading too, but he said he always felt smothered indoors, and knew he'd die if he had to spend his life working in an office.

Jim doesn't know if he should teach me all about building. He does anyway but he won't let me do anything much. I only get to help clean up, or hand people things, and not much of that. Jim thinks it's too dangerous. . . . He won't even let his work crews use nail guns. One guy let his nail gun slip and it drove a nail right through his hand. Another let his slip and it shot a nail clear across the room. It missed one of the other guys' heads by a hair. Now they only use nail guns when it's a big job and Jim's sure of his work crew.

Jim says when I'm older, and I do come up here and work summers, that maybe I should work for somebody else, not him. Lots of men's sons do that. They'd just rather work for Jim than for their own father. I think that's 'cause Jim is special, but he thinks it's because they're relatives. He says fathers and sons sometimes don't do things as well together as they would if they were strangers.

If my Dad was alive, we'd get along just fine. And I know I could work for Jim. . . . Rick works for his father. . . . I don't know if I could be a lawyer like my Dad was. . . .

I love Alaska and I'd like to live up there. I worry that I might be too much of a city person. I don't think I am, but if I am maybe I could live in Anchorage or Fairbanks.

9

Moose and Moose Berries

I told you a long time ago that Moose are exciting and interesting, but I never said they weren't ugly. I mean Ugly! They have long skinny legs, long droopy heads, and thick stiff fur that you wouldn't want for a fur coat, or even a rug. And they have a long piece of floppy skin and fur that hangs down on their neck. They are humped backed and beady eyed. And they stink. A hunter told me that in the fall when they get together and the bull moose fight each other over who gets the bunch of females, that they have a stink like you wouldn't believe! And they don't even fight fair. Two bulls can be fighting head on, and another one will come and attack one of them from the side.

Of course moose aren't just ugly. You really have to admire them too. They are big, and anything *that* big makes your mouth fall open just looking at them. And when they have a big set of antlers, it makes them look strong and grand, instead of funny looking. And even if they are funny looking, nature seems to have made them for Alaska. Their long skinny legs let them stand deep in ponds where they love to eat the stuff that's growing there. And they are great swimmers. Their stiff fur hairs are hollow, so they don't feel the cold much and it doesn't drag them down in the water.

Female moose seem to be good mothers. They have a lot of twins, and you see the twins with their mamas until they're quite big, maybe until they have their next twins.

Everybody knows that when you are out in the wild you never get between a mother animal and her babies. A moose will charge you, and even without antlers I guess a mama moose could kill you. I talked to one of the sales ladies in the Denali Park gift shop about the mother moose and calf that were hanging around the hotel up there. They were almost tame, just standing there chewing leaves and things. People were crowding around taking pictures. The picture takers weren't real close to the moose and baby, but a lot closer than you usually get. Anyway, the saleslady told me that some days when she's hurrying to work, cutting through the path in the woods there, she gets quite close to the mama moose before she knows it. But she always has to make herself stop and see where the baby is, or the mama might not act so tame.

Everybody up there likes moose. They are good eating. Lots of the natives get the meat all ground into burgers, or they get it made into moose wieners. Jim doesn't do much hunting, but lots of his friends give him moose meat, just like they give him fish they catch. Tourists like moose too. . . .

When moose go to the bathroom, they

make a neat package, like little eggs, but not pointed at the ends. We call them moose berries. Visitors buy real moose berries in the tourist shops. Honest! Usually there is varnish or something on them and they do all sorts of funny things with them. Sometimes they put them in the bottom of a cup, so you'd drink down and see it. Or they have them on top of a stick that you use to stir drinks. I know it's crazy, but people pay real money for moose berries, even just dried ones in a package. And they're not hard to find. On one abandoned road, near where me and Jim camped, we saw hundreds of them. It looked like the moose had used that road as their own private outhouse.

Moose don't usually bother you, except the hunter told me that bull moose get careless in the fall when they are after a harem of females, and then they get crazy. They'll attack you. They've killed hunters. They even attack trains that run from Anchorage to Fairbanks.

They look kind of dopey, though, like they wouldn't hurt you. One looked almost friendly to Uncle Jim years ago. It was when he first came to Alaska. My Dad went up there to visit him. This was before I was even born. Anyway, my Dad and Uncle Jim were out traveling around, looking the country over. They were way up north, heading for Circle, a town near the arctic circle. They got tired of driving and walked up a bluff that overlooked a pond. Just below them they saw a young female moose in the water, eating pond grasses. She looked pretty tame, and they started nudging each other. They were so tempted to jump down and land on her back and see if they could ride her.

My Dad and Jim grew up on a farm and had ridden cows and horses and mules and pigs and anything else they could find. It had been a joke with them about how many different animals they could ride on. Well, they both wanted to jump on that moose. They figured that if one of them tried it and got dumped right away, the other one was there to help, and they were both great swimmers. They kept poking each other, and daring each other. But they knew it was stupid, and tried to talk themselves out of it.

Well, that's what they finally did. They were grown men and it was just dumb to take a chance and try to ride a moose, even though they were tempted. They were always glad they didn't do it too, but I remember Dad talking about it. And even Jim says that he still thinks about it now and again.

Later, Jim heard a story that convinced him they were right never to get close to a moose, let alone try to ride one. It was early in the spring, and the snows had been very deep that winter. The snows melted first near the buildings, and moose would come and eat the green grass. One moose acted almost tame, coming right close to people so he could get that nice grass. Well, one dumb man asked a friend of his to take his picture while he kicked the moose. He thought it would be a funny picture. He didn't give the moose much of a kick, and the guy got the picture, but that was the end of the guy who kicked a moose. Without even turning around, the moose kicked back just as hard as he could. The man ended up in the hospital, and after a few days he died.

Well, you know, that just because something looks funny, and you joke about "berries," and it's like a big old cow and eats grass, doesn't mean you can tame it, or mess with it.

10

Glaciers

I don't like to talk about glaciers. It's like talking about God or something. Glaciers are special. There are hundreds of them in Alaska, but every one is special. They are snow turned to ice that's a few thousand years old. The snows were so thick and heavy that they pressed down and down, making a deep layer of ice. The snow that comes now piles up on that ice, but when summer comes only the top layer melts, so the glacier stays there.

Some glaciers move. They are like rivers of ice in high valleys between high mountains. They don't move fast, maybe only a foot a year, but when they move, they break off pieces that fall into lakes and rivers.

A piece of glacier ice that breaks off is called a "calf." I like that. It's like they are living things, like a moose or something.

Glaciers grind away at the hard stone on the mountains when they move. They grind the stone so fine that it gets like powder or flour. It is so light that it doesn't sink to the bottom in the rivers, but floats in them and makes them cloudy. Some water gets dirty . . . cloudy with dark glacier flour. Other water, dark blue rivers, turn turquoise from the flour, and that's one of the prettiest blues you can think of.

Blue is my favorite color. It's the color of sky and water. It's the color of Jim's eyes and Aunt Marge's, and Jane's, the girl who sits next to me in class. Mine are grey, darn it. . . . Glacier ice has streaks of blue. That's how you know it's a glacier. They say the ice is so dense it forms a prism and turns the ice blue. I know what a prism is. It's a piece of crystal that can change the way light moves. It can make rainbows on things when light hits it. But there aren't any rainbows in glaciers, just places that are a color of blue you don't see anywhere else. Like they trapped a special piece of the sky.

Of course some glaciers have ground up so much rock and dirt that even the tops of them have turned dark, and they become "black ice." You have to look carefully to even see those, because from a distance they look like the ground.

There are a lot of famous glaciers in Alaska that everybody goes to look at. And there are others so high and out of the way that you only get a little peek at them from a long way off. Some you don't get to see at all, unless you're in an airplane.

The Glacier near the airport in Juneau is named the Mendenhall Glacier. A lot of them have names that everyone knows. . . . I met a crazy, wild, really old lady in Juneau, who grew up not far from the Mendenhall Glacier. She was great. As old as she was, she was still rough and mouthy. She must have been something when she was young! Anyway, she told me that in the early days the saloons would get their ice from the Mendenhall Glacier. It was a kind of pride to have a drink made with glacier ice. . . . In her home, they would use chunks of it in their ice box. That was before home refrigerators. . . . She said that in the saloons they would have fights like you wouldn't believe! She laughed and said she thought there was special power in that ancient ice.

Nobody gets ice from the Mendenhall Glacier any more. You just look at glaciers and think about them. . . . A few you can walk on, but that's dangerous.

I've walked on glaciers. Mostly on the Matanuska Glacier. It was scary. There were big strange looking forms made out of black ice. I could hear water running, but I didn't see much of it at first. I felt cold from the ice, but the sun was warm on my hair. I walked toward the places where the ice stuck up in the air and was mostly blue. After a while I saw where the surface water was going through a hole, and I bent down and watched. There was a whole stream of fast moving water right underneath me. I didn't stay there long after that.

People who study glaciers are some kind of geologists. I'd like that kind of job. They figure out how fast a glacier is moving, and if it keeps on pushing down to the water. They know when it's breaking off so much that it's getting smaller. . . . The glacier near Portage is like that. The part where the calves break off used to be close, and now it's far across the lake, because so much broke off. The glacier looks small now, way across the water, but you should see some of the calves that break off. They are as big as a boat, because a lot of the glacier is already underwater.

I took a ferry trip with Rick and his mom last summer and we went to see the Columbia Glacier. The glacier goes back for miles over mountains and comes out at the water in a huge wall of ice. The ferry we were on went quite close, but not close enough to be very dangerous, unless the whole wall came down on you, which it never does. We went late in July and it was a warm day, but with all that ice wall, and so many broken off pieces of ice in the water all around us, the air suddenly got very cold.

Pieces break off the Columbia Glacier all the time. And a noise can start it off, just like an avalanche. Me and Rick went up where they let you blow the ferry whistle to send sound waves across the water to break pieces off the glacier. And it worked! Then we went down on the open deck and a bunch of us decided to shout together and see if that would bring the ice down. Sure enough, it did.

We hoped we'd see seals around the glacier. Sometimes there's lots of them. There were none in close that day but we could see them way off in the distance, sitting on the ice floes.

11

Places

If you look at a map of Alaska, you see that south of Anchorage is the Kenai Peninsula. That's where a lot of people live and a lot of people go. Right at the tip of the Peninsula is a town called Homer, and at the end, the tip of land beyond that, is called Homer spit. That's a great place. On one side is a skinny beach where you can pitch a tent and see mountains right across the water. . . . Mountains with snow even in the summer. And on the other side of the spit is the place where all the boats are docked, the marina. Mostly they're small fishing boats, but some are just for fun cruising. I like marinas with all the different kinds of boats, and their crazy reflections in the water. And all the different names people give boats. I even like the smell of the water, with the smell of fish. . . . when it isn't too fishy.

Seward is another town on the Peninsula that has a great marina, and has mountains just across the water.

And Clam Gulch is on the Peninsula too. I've been clamming lots of times. When the tide is out you walk along the wet sand looking for a small round circle that tells you a clam is down there. Then you grab a clamming shovel and dig like crazy. As soon as you start digging, the clam knows you are after him and he digs down deeper in the sand. Finally, when your hole is very deep, you reach down and feel around for the clam. I have to reach my whole arm, right up to my shoulder. And then lots of times the clams are too fast for you and they get away.

There are oil rigs in the water off the Kenai Peninsula, but most of the oil comes down the Alyeska pipeline. It comes across almost the whole state down from Prudhoe Bay to Valdez. You see the pipeline near the road when you drive down from Fairbanks. I like it, all big and silvery, snaking up and down the hills. I think it's great that they could even figure out how to build such a thing, and that it brings oil to the whole country.

Aunt Marge said she used to worry about them tearing up the land for the pipeline and ruining everything. Jim says the people did a good job on the pipeline without disturbing things much.... Jim doesn't like people in Washington, D. C. telling Alaskans what to do. Aunt Marge says that if people hadn't hollered all the time over everything, that they wouldn't have done such a good job with the pipeline. Jim says that if they hadn't hollered so much, it would have gone a lot faster and easier and just as good. Aunt Marge says.... Oh, what do I know? I don't say anything when those two get going at me from two sides.

Valdez is the town where the pipeline comes out. There is a monster of a big plant there where the pipeline ends and the oil is taken away in huge boats. Valdez was hurt bad when there was the Alaskan earthquake years ago. It's all built up now, but I wonder what will happen with all that oil if there is another one there, and another tidal wave.

Earthquakes cause tidal waves. A kid told me his father was on Kodiak Island when the earthquake hit. The water pulled back from the land like it had never done before. Then he knew that a tidal wave would come, and people were made to get out of there. But when it came, the kid's father was high up and he said that the tidal wave was like a moving mountain of water.

Every place in Alaska is a little different. . . . It all has mountains and valleys and things, but some places are flat farmland, and some are all woods. I went up to a town once called Livengood, and I expected it to be something special, but it wasn't much. It might be "livin' good" for some people, but there wasn't much there at all, and so far north I expect it gets awful cold. . . .

Aunt Marge and Jim sure don't agree on what livin' good is. She loves our apartment. She said she'd hate to have to worry about mowing grass and working in a garden. I don't suppose I really like taking care of Jim's garden. . . . Yes, I do. I grew the biggest cabbages and turnips one year. If I didn't look at them every day they'd have grown big without my even seeing it happen. Some vegetables like cabbage get huge up there.

A lot of the roads in Alaska are dirt roads. Some of the dirt ones are almost as smooth to drive a car on as a regular road. But paved or regular, it seems like they have to fix every single road every summer 'cause the winters are so hard. You can't go rushing around places. If there is a road crew working, sometimes you just have to stay and wait.

We talked to a man on a road crew to

pass the time, and he said he had a place right on the lake nearby.

"Must be nice livin' right on a lake, so you can step out your door and go fishing," Jim said.

"Oh, there ain't no fish in my lake," the man said. "I don't want there to be none. If there's fish, then you get people coming in boats and all, and they disturb the peacefulness. No, sir, I'm glad there's no fish in it."

Jim and me talked later about whether the man was lying to keep people from fishing out the place, but we finally allowed as how maybe an empty lake was his idea of living good, even if it wasn't ours.

Two interesting places are up near the Arctic Circle. One is called Circle, because I guess they thought they were on the circle when they built there, but it's not quite there. Far enough, though. We hit a rainstorm when we went up there and the dirt road was all torn up because they were widening it. Mud! It got so muddy we like to never have gotten out of there. If Jim wasn't so good with that old pick-up of his, we'd probably still be stuck in that mud.

Circle isn't much of a town, but it's great because it's right on the Yukon River. You drive into the tiny town, right up to the edge of the river, and it spreads out broad and fast and beautiful. It's a powerful river, and different in different places, like any great river. We walked up a ways and saw a fish trap in the water, down below the high bank. Nobody was going to rob that fish trap. There were several mean looking huskies guarding it.

There's a small local radio station in the town and a few houses. Maybe fifty people live there. Jim and me went inside the cafe, if you can call it that, and talked to the young guy at the cash register. He was from Texas and was already homesick although he had only been up there a few weeks. I guess most of the folks up there are natives and they are used to it.

Before leaving town we decided to drive

around the few streets. We were going along one rutted muddy street when I saw an open shed in someone's yard where they were drying their own smoked salmon. It was a big one and when Jim slowed down and then stopped so we could get a quick look. I leaped out of the car to take a picture. I wanted to tell Rick's mom about it and show her the picture. That was a mistake. Jim told me as I got out of the car that I better not, but I thought he just wanted to get going and make some miles before dark. Well, what happened is the old native woman who lived in the house saw me as I walked around trying to get the picture in focus. She came out and started hollering at me and waving her fist. I ran back to Jim's truck and got in fast. That didn't stop her and she hustled over toward the road still mad and saying things that I couldn't figure out.

Jim lit out of there fast. He didn't say anything to the woman except nod his head, and gestured toward me as if to say that I was just a kid and didn't know any better.

"Why is she so mad, Jim?" I asked as we pulled away. I turned and looked back and she was still shaking her fist, still saying things we couldn't hear.

"Oh, she thinks we're tourists," Jim said. "She probably thinks we're making fun of her drying her own fish. Or that we're just nosy and careless. She has a right to her privacy. We're the ones who were wrong."

"Well, why didn't you explain? We're not the kind to make fun. She's got a great set-up there."

"She didn't want explanations. We'd have only made it worse," Jim said. "We shouldn't have gone there and that's that."

"You mean I shouldn't have gotten out of the car. You tried to stop me."

"Well, you learned something. No harm done," Jim said.

We were both quiet after that and headed down a road pointing to Arctic

Circle Hot Springs. That's a tourist place, but a nice one. They've got a hotel there and they're fixing up some old buildings that are going to be pretty nice. I guess they used to be log cabins for tourists in the old days. The hotel was built in 1930. It says it up over the door. The top floor has little rooms made like tents that you have to stoop to get into. They call them hostel rooms and we got one and used our own sleeping bags. We had dinner there too. Jim said we were going to be comfortable one night and feast instead of having the mosquitos feast on us.

The dinner was all homemade and you could eat all you wanted to. Jim had liver and onions and everything else. I settled for just salmon, salad, potatoes, and tons of homemade bread, still hot.

We ate early, put our gear in the hostel room, roamed around a bit to let our supper settle and then went swimming. There's a swimming pool right next to the hotel that gets its water from a natural hot spring. The water comes out of the ground so hot it almost burns you.

We both went swimming in the pool and it was too hot to stay near the place where the water poured in. You had to get way out in the middle where the air cooled it, and then it felt good. It started to rain a little, but it didn't matter. We had done enough camping in the rain and mud with mosquitos eating us alive. Swimming in the hot pool in the cool rain, that was living good. . . .

Those hot springs must have felt even better to the gold miner who first discovered them years and years ago. He, or someone like him, put the springs to good use too. They put tents over the springs and men would pay to go in and bathe, or just get all warm and steamy. Sometimes the outsides of the tent would freeze so hard they had to chop the ice off to get in.

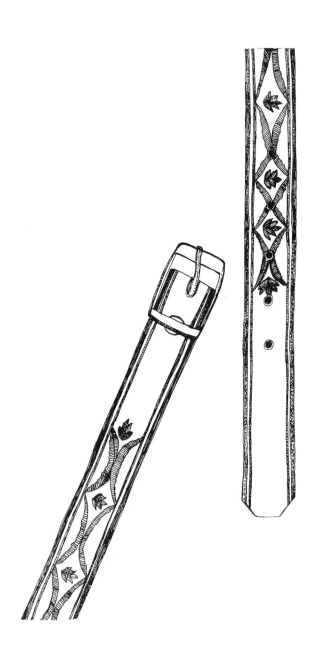

12

People

People in Alaska are different from other people. Everybody says this and it's true. They see life differently. In fact, you're going to think I'm crazy, but when they talk and stare off into space it's like they are seeing things. . . . seeing themselves, their lives, the country. . . . I don't know how to explain it. Jim says there are mostly two kinds up there . . . those who are running away from something and those who are trying to find something. He likes both kinds, and maybe everybody is a little bit of both, but mostly he likes people who are in Alaska to find something about themselves. People who love the place like he does. If people are just running away from something, they end up just taking themselves with them and it's themselves they don't like.

Alaskans don't chatter away at you like I do. Most of them talk kinda slow, sort of all around a subject before they sink their teeth in it. Maybe they've seen a lot of animals do that, look things over carefully before moving in. I'm not saying that they can't or won't talk once they get going. Everybody has a tale to tell, they just want to tell it in their own way and to the folks that will appreciate it.

I'm a good listener. I don't really talk all the time. I've heard all the hunting stories and fishing stories, and bear stories, and the women tell them just as good as the men.

Alaskan artists are fun to talk to. I guess it's because they train their eyes to notice everything. One artist, the one who drew the picture of the eagle that Jim has, draws lots of eagles. He lives down near Haines and that's a favorite place for seeing eagles because after the salmon spawn, the dead ones flow downstream and lay in the water. For some reason the water doesn't freeze solidly there in the fall and hundreds of eagles come to feed.

Some of the eagles stay there year round and the artist watches them and gets to know them and how they act. One he called "The Neighbor" because he was such a busybody, turning his head, watching everything that went on around him. He would watch the cars and the people and seemed to forget he was an eagle. Another was "The Watcher," but he was a smart fisherman who watched the bay. And the "Dumb Fisherman" was a clown of a bird who didn't know his own abilities. He'd get fish that were too big and drop them. He'd even get run off by the gulls.

Jim has pictures by another artist that are also great! He does mostly animals, but animals with a whole scene around them so you are almost in the snowstorm where two elk are fighting, or can feel the white frosty breath coming from the mouths of grizzlies. This artist lives in the wilderness and comes to town only when he needs money for food or clothes. But Jim worries about him because he's losing his sight, and then how will he survive?

Some of the old timers you meet had parents who lived to be old timers too. So things we read about only in books they heard first hand. One old lady had a father who had been in Oklahoma before it was a state. He was in the line when the Cherokee Strip was opened up. That was when they decided that people could get free land if they would race to where they wanted it and put stakes down and claim it as their own. They all lined up in a huge long line. A gun was shot off and they raced across the prairie on horseback and with wagons like crazy rushing to get the spot they'd picked out before someone else got it. The only thing was, some people cheated and sneaked in and put down the marking stakes ahead of time. They were called "Sooners" because they went in too soon.

Anyway, her father and his brother got this land and started a farm but he soon got tired of farming. After a couple years he gave it to his brother. He had done it for the adventure. Then, when he heard that gold was discovered in the Klondike he figured he'd head up there. He was all set to get married too, but he promised the girl that he'd come back for her. She said he'd never come back and that she was going with him, married or not. That was the mother of the lady who told me the story.

Well, they did get married but by the time they got to Skagway in Alaska so many people had already tried and failed to get rich, been killed by an avalanche, or starved out that they decided to stay in Skagway and set up a small business. She did sewing and he made things of leather at first. Then they tried different businesses. They stayed in Skagway and had eight children. The lady I talked to was the youngest and the only one still alive, because the gold rush was way back in 1898.

It's funny how you get to talking to people. The day I met the old lady Jim was talking business to someone down at the dock in Skagway and I went wandering around by myself. I saw this little house with a garden and it was such a pretty garden I took a picture of it for Aunt Marge. I feel like I have to keep showing Aunt Marge that Alaska has some pretty civilized places too. Anyway, I was standing on the lady's lawn concentrating on making it a good picture and I never heard her come near me until after I snapped the picture.

"I hope it's a good one," she said.

Of course I apologized for getting on her property and explained the picture was for Aunt Marge. I felt stupid because she could have been as angry at me as the old native woman.

"Don't you like the garden for yourself, too?" she asked. Her old eyes crinkled up and sparkled when she said that and I got all flustered and embarrassed.

"A man should never be ashamed of liking pretty things," she said.

And then she invited me inside and gave me a glass of milk and homemade bread thick with butter. She showed me leather-work her father had done and it was beautiful. He had carved flowers into the leather. That's when she told me about him and the Cherokee Strip . . . and her mother wanting to follow him to Alaska and all that. The family had stayed in Skagway and this old lady had married the son of a man who'd come looking for gold. He was dead now and her children were all grown up and gone, but she stayed on by herself because she loved it there.

But I wasn't going to tell you about Skagway yet. I wanted to tell you about an old man I met on the ferry coming up the inside passage, on the same boat when I met David, the one who worked in fossil ivory. It was getting rainy and cold one day in the solarium so I went and found a seat on another deck in the front of the ship where you can watch the ship move its way along the passage between the islands. There was an old man sitting next to me who watched that water and land as if he was personally in charge of steering the boat himself. It didn't take long to figure out why. He told me he was a fisherman and had traveled the passage up and back for 34 years. He knew every inch of the water and he showed me things I'd have never noticed by myself. He showed me whales that he could spot even in the rain, and that other people sitting there hadn't even seen. He pointed out a young eagle, that I wouldn't have known was a bald eagle because its head feathers hadn't turned white yet. But he knew just by the way it flew and its size.

He didn't talk steady once he got started, like most people do. He kept getting quiet, looking at the water and the outlines of the land.

Finally, when he was real quiet, but was squinting as though he was seeing something, I asked him what he saw this time that I didn't see.

He laughed. "Oh, you see everything that's there. I'm just seeing what used to be there. See that place, just ahead, where there's no rock, no anything to block the channel? Well, I'm remembering the rock that used to be there. It was dangerous. Caused a current that crashed many a boat. Almost crashed on it myself once. There were a lot of ideas for getting rid of that rock, lots of things tried I expect. We're off the Canadian coast. The Canadian government finally drilled into that rock and put in hundreds of thousands of pounds of dynamite. They blew it all up at once. It was an amazing job. Dangerous, expensive, but it worked. Water runs through there now just as smooth and nice as you please."

He told me things about fishing too.

. . . I don't want you to think that everyone up there is old with old tales. That's not really true. Jim knows one kid who used to be the wildest kid, getting into trouble all the time. Jim hired him, trusted him, and taught him. The kid took to roofing like a duck to water. He was just a natural. Jim helped him set up his own business. He's twenty-two and has his own roofing business and is doing fine.

Jim knows another man in his thirties. He had been married and divorced. He kept their son because his wife didn't care, but then she changed her mind and stole the man's car and his son and drove from California to Virginia to live. Well, the man didn't have another car and he wanted his son, but he didn't have the money to go chasing after them. So he started working two jobs, bought a motor-cycle and rode clear across the country and stole his eight year old son right back. Picked him up on the way home from school.

By then it was summertime so the father hired a lady to watch his son and started working and saving again. But he couldn't find a good job and he worried the whole time that his wife would come looking for him and his son again. He wanted to go to Alaska where his wife couldn't find him and where a friend promised him work, but he knew it was stupid to take a chance on the Alaskan highway with just a motorcycle. Actually, he knew all about motorcycles and how to repair them so he and his son finally went on the motorcycle. They didn't have any problems either. He was hired by a friend of Jim's and I've seen him and his son too.

13

Gold

People still pan and dig for gold in Alaska. There were people working along the river most of the way to Circle. There's not lots of gold like in the early days, but I guess that now that gold costs a lot, it's worth it to work the old claims. At least some folks seem to think so.

When Jim and me saw on the map that the road to Dawson was one we hadn't been on, we decided to go there and then follow the roads down from Dawson to Skagway. That's the route the miners took, only they went from Skagway to Dawson. That's called the Trail of '98. It goes mostly through Canada. In fact, Dawson is in Canada. So is a town called White Horse.

When I said that Alaska is exciting today and people shouldn't think everything happened in the old days, I didn't mean that it isn't exciting to go see places that are full of history. I just meant that isn't the ONLY thing to do. But going to places where there is a lot of history can stir you up good. . . .

You have to take a ferry to cross the Yukon River to get to Dawson City. The Yukon is a long way from the ocean when you get to Dawson, but salmon come way up that far. Salmon always return from the ocean to where they were born, and if they were born near Dawson, that's where they swim to.

I read that "Klondike" was originally pronounced "Trond-deg," and was the Indian word for "hammerwater." That's because in the old days wooden stakes were hammered into the river to trap salmon. And the word "Yukon" was the Indian word meaning "Greatest River."

We went on the riverboat that's on the

river bank at Dawson, and it shows you what the old paddle wheelers were like. . . . Do you know how much wood a cord of wood is? Well, it's quite a pile. They used to burn a cord of wood in one hour to get up the steam to move that paddlewheeler. They could fit six cords of wood on the boat and it would go for six hours before having to stop and get another load of wood.

The boat had little bedrooms so people could sleep on it. They weren't fancy, but it was still a boat for rich people. Most people looking for gold up at Dawson couldn't afford to take the paddlewheeler. And the beds were little. People must have been small in the old days. Jim could never fit in a short bed like those.

Past the town of Dawson was Bonanza Creek, where a lot of the gold was found. It's a place to give you the shivers. There's nothing there but a few rusted steam engines and piles of rocks. The rocks are called "tailings." That's all the stuff that was dug out of the creek when they looked for gold. And the piles are still there, miles of them, with hardly anything growing on them. They show how the men dug and sweat to get the gold they got.

Way on down from Dawson is a place where the river is very dangerous. There is an island in the middle that the paddle-wheelers could have gotten wrecked on. Well, they had that problem figured out good. In the old days they had the machinery and cables set up so that the boats could be sort of pulled and guided through the water from the land.

They had good ideas in those days. And great names for people. The men who found the first gold were two Indians and a white man. The Indians were called Skookum Jim and Tagish Charley. The white man was George Washington Carmack. Later, in Skagway, there was a bad man who tried to run the town and his nickname was Soapy. Soapy Smith. They do a show about him and about how Frank

Reid killed him. Reid got killed doing it, though.

When we drove to Skagway we saw the train that was built to get the miners over the pass. I don't know how they ever built a railroad on the edge of mountains like that, but they did it. And it's still running.

You learn all sorts of things in places like Skagway. They have a small museum crammed with stuff. But it makes you sad. "Dead Horse Gulch" sounds like a good old name, but over three thousand horses and other animals died going over White Pass. Boy, that place must have stunk!

The miners went through things that are hard to believe. There were murders and suicides, deaths from the cold, and avalanches. . . . one killed over sixty people.

Aunt Marge told me one time that TV and newspapers stir people up too much about the wrong things. I guess newspapers always did that. A newspaper article in 1897 said 68 miners came to Seattle on the boat from Alaska with suitcases, sacks, and jars of gold that weighed a ton! That stirred everybody up and caused the gold rush that killed so many men. But what can newspapers do? And you know what? When they actually weighed the gold, the newspaperman hadn't been exaggerating at all. It actually weighed two tons! That's a lot of gold!

Jim never panned for gold much, except a little bit now and then, mostly for fun. He says the whole country is gold. He means it's a great place to live.

The best part of our trip to Skagway didn't have anything to do with sight-seeing and history. It was seeing the sculptor, David, in Skagway. He's the guy I told you I met on the ferry from Seattle. He's the one who gave me a piece of scrimshaw for showing him around Ketchikan.

Anyway, there's me and Jim walking down the street in Skagway. It was late and almost dark. We had set up our tent at the campground and were just walking down the street, hoping to find some places open, because it was too early to go to bed.

I had my head down and I was looking in the store windows when I saw that carved bird that David had made, the one with the wings back and streaks of grey in the wings. I figured David had let the store sell it for him, but I didn't expect to see him. I looked up, and there he was working at a big old desk, right inside his own store. When we went inside I was afraid David wouldn't recognize me, and for a few seconds he didn't, because he was so deep in thought from the carving he was doing. But then he remembered and I introduced him to Jim and everything was great.

Sometimes, people you like a lot don't like each other. I don't know why. Aunt Marge says that happens to her all the time. She says that any more she doesn't even try to get one friend to like another friend. . . . Aunt Marge and Jim don't like each other hardly, even if they don't say it. And they wouldn't like each other at all if they saw each other much.

David isn't anything like Jim. He's kinda

short, and he talks a lot, and he likes cities and people. Lots of his sculptures are abstracts, not real things like Jim likes. But David is an Alaskan in other ways. I don't know how to say it. He's willing to take a risk. . . . to be his own man, like Jim. . . . I can't explain it, but it was important to me for them to like each other. . . . I suppose because I still worried about whether I was a city person like my Dad or an outdoor person like Jim. I know Jim worried about that too. Dad was a lawyer. He wore suits and neckties. And if that was the way I was supposed to be then Jim didn't want to make me into something else.

Anyway, you know what? Jim and David got along just fine! David showed us the big desk he was working on and said it was borrowed. It was one that a miner had shipped all the way to Skagway. Then he showed us the stuff he was selling, and told all about how he landed in Skagway after missing the folks he was supposed to see in Juneau. And how he set up his own store, and painted it and made partitions. He closed the store for us that night and we went down the street to the Red Onion Saloon. They had drinks and I had a coke and they talked a lot. They told tales and I could tell that they liked each other.

When we finally left and walked back up the street toward David's store, Jim asked him about the gold chains he had for sale in the window. I guess Jim was thinking about buying one for his girlfriend.

"Those chains, they're bait for the Russians," David said.

"I don't get it," I said.

"Well, I always wanted to meet Russians," David said. "I can't speak Russian or anything, but I thought it would be nice if they came in my store. Skagway is only one of two ports where Russian sailors come on their ships and wander around town. They never come in my studio because they aren't interested in fossil ivory. They don't seem to know it's rare and valuable. . . . So, I got some gold chains.

Russians buy gold and maybe that's just the right bait to get them in there and get to know them.

Jim thought that was great. His laughter boomed loud. He was having a good time and he laughed and laughed. But he was quiet later when we walked back to the campground. We crawled in our sleeping bags and got ready to sleep.

Then Jim said, "Your friend David is okay." He said it like he'd been doing some serious thinking.

I'd been thinking too. I decided I'm not going to worry any more about what type of person I'll be. I'll be an Alaskan. There's all kinds of good men in Alaska . . . city people and country people . . . men in white shirts and flannel shirts. There will be one more good man there when I'm grown up.